HER ETERNAL LOVE

MARIA CHRISTINE

A NOCTURNA PRESS BOOK

Her Eternal Love
Second Edition
Copyright 2020 Maria Christine

Original Copyright 2011

Cover and Interior design by Nocturna Press
Front cover illustration by Andrejs Pidjass, Getty Images
(edited by Nocturna Press)
Back cover illustration by Claws by Pialhovik. Getty Images
(edited by Nocturna Press)

Nocturna Press
Independence, Missouri
www.NocturnaPress.com

ISBN-13: 978-1-944673-32-1 (paperback)
ISBN-13: 978-1-944673-33-8 (e-book)

Library of Congress Control Number: 2019939516

Published in the United States of America

her eternal love

PROLOGUE

Elena sat atop the highest rock staring out upon the splendid view. An amethyst cloak shielded her soft caramel skin from the cool mountain breeze. She fixed her gaze upon the glorious range and vast rain forest below, and she pondered. It had been ten years. Ten years since her nineteenth birthday—the night she'd danced in the woods with her friends until the midnight hour. A decade since she'd changed—or rather, when someone changed her—into a vampire.

For years, she avoided contact with ordinary humans in effort to stay her thirst. She didn't want to harm anyone, and the blood of non-magical beings was nearly irresistible. Over the years she'd learned to feast on the nectar of fruits and even flowers. Lately, however, she felt different. Something inside was beginning to erupt. It was a craving; a hunger she'd suppressed for many years yet was beginning to beckon her against any restraint she might have.

This wasn't a thirst for blood; it was different. Elena knew exactly what it was, and tried desperately to shake it to no avail. She had to have Decio. She felt his pulse nearby. Not the pulse of a beating heart, but the pulse of his beating soul. And he felt hers too.

her eternal love

CHAPTER One

R arely in a vampire's everlasting life does he feel such emotion, but Elena and Decio shared a bond; an unyielding connection that burned in their hearts like a roaring flame yet could never be satisfied. They could not be together for it was forbidden—forbidden by the keeper of the tenet; daughter of Lucifer and wife of the emperor, Imperial Lord LaVius, ruler of the Seventh Dimension. She was known by many names, among them Empress Domnina, governor of the Realm of Shadows.

The rules set by the empress were never to be questioned, and no one ever dared to pass the thought. It had been the natural way of things for centuries. In fact, the empress regarded Elena's family as her own, and before falling in love with Decio, Elena never questioned the governor's decisions. Elena indeed stayed away as instructed, but her heart ached for him. And as her hunger for Decio increased, the more determined she became to find out why they were ordered to stay apart.

M'Shara, the wise mystic of the woods, was Elena's mother and a fierce friend to the empress. She had untold powers and superior clairvoyance. She knew the truth behind the separation of Elena and Decio but felt that explanation was not necessary; the rules were set and that was enough. But she also knew that her daughter was nearby. Her senses told her that Elena was returning to the realm and would inevitably—against all council and reason—confront the governor.

The woods were murky and cool. M'Shara sat at the round oak table in her cottage, staring into the pool of her scrying bowl. As the ripples in the water settled, her own reflection: dark brown skin and deep purple eyes, began to fade and the image of her daughter became clear. She saw what Elena was planning, and she knew the dangerous aftermath that would follow those actions. She was shaken. Her nails gripped the table. She had to do something right away. She had to get to the empress before her daughter had a chance. She slipped under a black cloak and rushed to her horse. There was not a moment to lose.

CHAPTER TWO

As she neared the land that housed the black citadel, palace of the emperor and empress, M'Shara felt a distinct chill. She was definitely close. Dusk was fading into night and she could not see the fortress, but there were watchers that would know she approached. She would be welcomed, but was on her guard. As she rode through the woods at high speed, she knew that many eyes were upon her, though she could see none. She threw back her hood so the unseen guards would recognize her and hold their positions. They let her pass. Word however, did reach the palace long before M'Shara reached the gates. They opened as she approached. She never slowed down.

Outside, the palace was dark, forbidding, and its basalt walls were cool to the touch. Inside, it was warm. Red rugs adorned the stone floors and stairs, and enormous fireplaces were in every room including the front entry. Inside them, the flames seemed to come from the depths somewhere beneath the floor, possibly underground.

LaVius and Domnina were in the dining hall. He was just finishing a rich meal of boar and sour bread, and she stood behind him dressed in red velvet, her hands firmly massaging his neck as he ate. LaVius had skin of ivory and hair that flowed like a river of silk past his powerful shoulders. Domnina's skin was warm olive and smooth, and was radiant in the muted light. Her dark hair was swept up regally, and her lips matched her gown, as did the very large inferno ruby ring that adorned her marriage finger. It warmed her hand whenever magical beings neared. She smiled when she was alerted to M'Shara's arrival.

"She nears, my dear LaVius."

"Yes, I could feel her heartbeat some time ago," he answered as he wiped his mouth with a cloth then dropped it on the table.

The empress slid around to his side and both drank the red wine from their cups. M'Shara was announced, and at the nod of the dark lord, she was allowed to enter. LaVius groaned as he swallowed the liquid. Although he too was fond of M'Shara—and he wasn't fond of many—he knew something of M'Shara's business with them this night. He simmered silently and waited for her to begin. The empress was not as aware at the moment. She ushered her friend into the room and embraced her. "M'Shara, come in. Have something to eat."

"Thank you. No," M'Shara answered.

"Then a drink? I insist," the empress pressed. "Sit here. I'll pour."

A male servant came in, but Domnina insisted on pouring the wine. He cleared the table and brought LaVius something stronger to drink.

M'Shara seemed a bit uncomfortable and LaVius noticed at once. He looked at her intently but didn't give away what he knew. "You seem troubled M'Shara," he said. "Come now. Tell us what is on your mind."

The empress's back stiffened when she heard his tone. Her eyes darted to her friend. "M'Shara?" she asked. "Why have you come?"

M'Shara breathed deeply and began. "It is true. Something weighs on my mind. I come to you as a friend. I must ask something of you, and I beg you will see reason."

The governor's eyes began to darken. M'Shara held the goblet in her hand and began to swirl the wine. She tried to compose herself. LaVius watched his wife with tongue in cheek.

Empress Domnina stood firmly. She was not always a patient person. "Do you wish to tell me what is on your mind, M'Shara?"

M'Shara stilled the wine and gazed up at her sinister-looking friend. "It's Elena," she blurted.

LaVius knew as much. He grinned slyly and chuckled to himself as he took a drink, but never looked up from his goblet.

The empress closed her eyes and turned away. "M'Shara," she began as she stared into the burning fireplace. "Does this have anything to do with her return?" She was sure of the truth, yet still bothered to hope she was wrong. She didn't want M'Shara to ask what she was about to.

M'Shara stood from her chair. "Then you knew she was back?"

"Of course," Domnina replied, her back ever turned. "Well?" she tittered. "What is bothering you?"

"It is about Decio."

The empress's eyes shot sharply to her friend. "Decio? You know that what is done, is done. Furthermore, you know why they must remain apart."

"Yes," M'Shara breathed. "I know better than anyone. But please hear me out. I did not come here to change your mind. I agree they must stay parted, but my daughter has been gone a long while. She has returned, and I have foreseen the reason. They are drawn to each other—more than ever before. Their souls beckon each other and she is no longer able to stay away. She has decided to confront you."

Domnina's look became harsh. "You know how that will end. As does your daughter."

"That is why I have come, to beg for your favor," said M'Shara.

"I will not disregard her insolence," said

Domnina.

"You must!" M'Shara grabbed her friend's sleeve. "Please!"

The empress was truly taken aback. M'Shara had never been like this. She pondered a few thoughts. "M'Shara, I like to think of myself as reasonable and tolerant—"

M'Shara knew this not to be true, but agreed aloud. LaVius seemed amused. The empress looked his way shrewdly and finished her remarks. "My friend, we have known each other for nearly an age. I will carefully consider your request, and you will be made aware of my decision when the time comes."

M'Shara smiled charily. She knew there was nothing more she could ask.

The empress then handed M'Shara her drink and took her own goblet to her lips. "Let us drink."

They both sipped the Mourvèdre wine and LaVius stood from the table. He towered over M'Shara and he took her hand. "The solstice ball is in two nights. Please say you'll be in attendance."

"I would never miss it," she replied.

He bowed his head to her politely, and she did in return.

Empress Domnina drank her wine and pondered Elena once more. Her ring burned like fire against her skin. She knew who was nearby. She grinned but made no mention. Her husband took her gently by the neck with one hand and softly kissed her there. Her tensions simultaneously drifted away. He then left the women in order to attend to other business.

M'Shara shared more wine with the empress, but they spoke no more of Elena. Later, when she rode away into the dark forest, she could feel that her daughter was close.

Elena sat perched high on the branch of a giant kauri tree and watched her mother leave the castle. She would confront the empress at the solstice ball. But first, she would go to see Decio.

CHAPTER THREE

Now home, M'Shara sat in her wooden rocking chair staring through the open window into the darkness. As she rocked forward and back slowly, she was content with how things had gone with her friend. They shared a secret. And she hoped that Domnina would not reveal it to Elena. She was concerned, but less than before. She had to believe that her old friend would come through. She was concerned, but less than before. She had to believe that her old friend would come through.

In the dark castle, the lord and empress rested in their chamber. The only light was that of the fireplace. It was hot against LaVius's back as Domnina kneaded his shoulders. She stared at her ruby ring and thought about the situation. LaVius could feel her grip increase and knew that she was brooding. "Domnina," he spoke in a low, rumbling tone.

"Yes, my lord," she whispered.

"Do not be troubled by this. You will make the right decision." He turned around and sat up to face her.

She stared into his malevolent but endearing eyes. "You have such faith in me," she stated.

"Yes, my wicked and lovely woman. You've never failed to do what is best for the realm."

"But this decision is particularly difficult," she replied.

His voice quietly boomed. "No. There is but one possible decision. You know what must be done."

The empress turned away, but LaVius gripped her chin tightly and forced her to face him. "Don't forget who you are," he warned.

She leaned upward and met him incitingly

nose to nose. "Don't you forget either," she growled.

To which he replied with a proud and satisfied grin. "That's my vicious bride," he said and then kissed her waiting mouth.

CHAPTER FOUR

Miles from the castle, in the village of Redway, Elena strolled down the dirt road straight through town. It was late and most people were sleeping, but she knew there were those who preferred the night. She was after one in particular. She wore her cloak tight, the hood drawn so no one could see her face. She neared the end of the dirt lane and saw a familiar house in the distance. At the barn a light could be seen. As she neared it, she felt a vibration within her. It wouldn't be long. They would be together at last.

When she reached the edge of the huge

property, she threw her hood back and began to sprint. Her speed was paralleled by very few other vampires. She arrived at the barn in an instant. It was lined with stables. She slipped off her cloak and tossed it to the ground. She could smell him. She could almost taste him. As she slowly entered the barn, she observed lighted torches on the walls. The horses began to whinny and kick. They were nervous as she neared. But she was not there for them. She stood still in the middle of the barn and they hushed abruptly. She cocked her head to the side and he pounced onto the ground behind her. It was Decio.

She faced him at once and they stared at one another for several moments, gauging each other, pervading each other's essence, making certain it was not a dream. She'd longed to feel him; his alabaster skin, the muscles of his chest, the safeness of his arms around her. They had been apart too long. Each often wondered if the other had moved on, but knew in their hearts the truth. No words were needed. They suddenly embraced and their mouths were joined at last. Neither could withstand another moment apart. They would be together evermore, and no one could stop them.

Decio took Elena by the hand and led her to a ridge at the top of the hill. They sat in silence for a time, holding each other and memorizing each other's faces in the moonlight. All they'd ever wanted was this: to simply be together. It had been forbidden for what seemed an eternity, and they tried to abide by the order, but it was futile. Their hearts would not allow it.

"Elena, my beautiful woman, you are all I've ever wanted." Decio was overcome with emotion. He cupped her face with his hands. "I have dreamed of this moment all of these long years. I have tried, but I cannot survive without you. We must be together now at any cost."

"I feel the same. You are my one and only love, Decio. That is why I will confront the empress at the solstice ball, and tell her that we will be together no matter the consequences."

"Elena, you can't—"

"Yes, I can. And I will. I don't want us to be a secret. I won't run scared."

He smiled and stroked her cheek. "All right. Then we shall go together, and we will demand an explanation."

Elena smirked. "I don't care for her explanations."

"Don't you want to know why this all came to pass?" Decio asked.

"No. All I need to know is that you are with me, and that no one can keep us apart any longer."

He looked into her eyes proudly and lovingly. "I am with you, my love. I am with you forever."

CHAPTER FIVE

The night of the solstice ball had arrived, and the gates to the black citadel were open. Hundreds of creatures were in attendance and gathered on the grounds outside the castle. Many varieties of persons were there, both wicked and virtuous, dubious and upright. They set aside their differences to draw together and celebrate the holiday.

The gathering was a blend magical and non-magical beings of many species—some mortal, some immortal. Even though they laughed and sang and danced, ate their feast and enjoyed the festivities, there was a strangeness in the air. It was felt by all, and the crowd stirred with speculation.

M'Shara nervously awaited her daughter's arrival. She knew it would happen tonight. It was just a matter of when. Two familiar wolves slinked through the raucous crowd and past the fire-eaters. They approached M'Shara and shape-shifted into their human forms. They were her married friends, Devlin and Luna.

"What troubles you, our good friend?" Devlin asked. "Is it the sky this night? The look of it certainly troubles me."

"Yes, and me as well," Luna added. "Something about it is unorthodox. And the forest is too quiet."

M'Shara smiled at her friends, but did not reveal what was on her mind. She laughed to throw them off and to lighten the mood. "Well, the forest is quiet because all of the beasts are here," she said.

"Indeed, you are right," Devlin chuckled.

M'Shara wanted to cut the conversation short so they wouldn't pick up on her continuing anxiety and question her again. So, she bid them a fine evening and slipped away to find Domnina.

In fact, to M'Shara's perplexity, neither the empress nor Lord LaVius had made an appearance yet. She decided to look for them. She crossed the courtyard, went through the crowd, and started up the stone staircase which led to their thrones.

As she arrived midway up the staircase, the music suddenly stopped and the crowd gasped and murmured. M'Shara halted abruptly and turned around to see what the commotion was about. The crowd parted as Elena and Decio, dressed entirely in white, but in formal gala attire, sauntered up the walkway, their arms linked. Everyone there was in shock and stared in trepidation.

M'Shara's eyes fell upon her daughter and her eyes widened. She wanted to run and embrace her, but desperately wished she'd not made such a bold appearance. She swallowed hard and considered whether she could whisk Elena away before the empress and lord could see her. But her daughter was a grown woman. And furthermore, deep inside, she knew it was too late.

She was right. Simultaneously, two horns

began to sound; one deeper than the other. Elena smiled defiantly as she held onto Decio's arm. She held her head high as the newest arrivals were announced. The crowd looked onward up the staircase past M'Shara as they appeared.

What timing the empress had. M'Shara knew it was no coincidence. She closed her eyes, turned around slowly and exhaled. This was it.

LaVius and the empress appeared arm in arm at the top of the stairs. They were dressed regally in black and silver. Although an intimidating presence, LaVius was magnificently handsome. His long hair, the color of jet, urbanely blanketed his shoulders. His look was severe as everyone kneeled. He was ruler of the entire dimension and was feared and respected by all. Elena and Decio did kneel out of respect, but Elena stood up before anyone else. The empress took note of this. As everyone began to stand, she let go of her husband's arm and began to descend the stairs.

LaVius sat silently on his throne. M'Shara watched her friend intently. Her anxiety was at its peak. She was willing use her powers to defend her daughter, if need be, even though she knew the cost would be her own life. She hoped it wouldn't come to that.

The empress stood still on the center of the stairs in front of the hushed crowd. The train of her gown laid over the steps like a black river over fallen stones. She folded her hands. Her ring burned strongly due to the great deal of magical guests in attendance, but it was harmless to her.

She spoke in a condescending tone. "Good evening, Elena. It has been far too long since I've laid eyes on you. I am glad you have bestowed your presence upon us, and yet I see you've brought an interesting guest."

M'Shara stepped down a few stairs so that she could see Domnina's face when she spoke, and so that she would be more between her friend and her daughter.

Elena stepped forward to answer the empress's greeting. She was short in her words, as M'Shara had expected. "Thank you, Empress, for the welcome, but I didn't come here to exchange pleasantries."

The crowd gasped. LaVius narrowed his eyes. Empress Domnina only grinned. "You're a brazen young woman, but I suppose it is in your blood. Tell me, Decio, are you feeling as bold?"

Decio raised his head high and straightened his back. "I do not wish to disrespect you, governor, but wish to support Elena to the nth degree. We are in love."

The crowd began to murmur. LaVius rubbed his temple as a headache began. He then stood and cleared the crowd with one wave of his hand. Every single uninvolved soul exited the courtyard.

"Is this true, Elena?" Domnina asked.

"You know very well that it is," she spat. "I am deeply in love with Decio. We will never again be parted, and there is nothing you can do about it. At the full moon, we shall be married."

M'Shara nearly collapsed, but held a firm grip on the stone banister. Empress Domnina slowly met M'Shara's gaze. "I've heard enough, Elena," she said.

"No, you haven't. I'm not finished," Elena retorted. "I want you to stay away from us. You have kept us apart for nothing. Your inane laws have caused us nothing but heartache, and you've enjoyed every minute of it."

"Silence!" the empress demanded and flung her hand into the air to make her point. "This insolence is beneath you, and unlike you. It seems that love has clouded your judgment. Because of this, you have been allowed a bit of rope... but be wary of the noose at the end."

Decio grabbed Elena by the arm and quickly pulled her back. He tried to calm her.

The empress began to retreat up the stairs. Once there, she turned around and looked at them. "I am not required to explain my laws, but I too have feelings." She didn't look very believable, but was telling the truth. "I do not enjoy keeping you two apart, not when you love so deeply. But it is for a good cause."

M'Shara swallowed hard and stepped forward on the stair toward her friend. Her eyes pleaded with her not to reveal their secret.

The empress continued, regardless. "There is a secret I have kept from you both."

M'Shara tightened her eyes and dropped to one knee on the step. This was the moment she'd hoped would never come.

"It is difficult for me to say these words. They have been locked in my mind for a long while." Empress Domnina sat down on her throne next to LaVius and placed her hand on his. "It has been foretold that Decio will be married to one of my own kin. On the wedding night, he will destroy her… and I will destroy him."

Elena and Decio stared at her, their mouths loose with misunderstanding. But neither was more shocked than M'Shara who immediately raised her head to look at Domnina in disbelief. For the empress had told only part of the secret— and revised the rest.

Elena and Decio didn't understand. "Empress, what does this have to do with us?" Elena asked. Her tone was calmer than before and somewhat shaky.

"Yes, please tell us why this concerns us," Decio pleaded. "I am in love with Elena. She is no relation to you."

M'Shara braced herself while a second secret was revealed.

"You are quite wrong, Decio," Domnina said. "Elena is the daughter of my brother, Kane."

Elena's eyes grew wide. "You're lying!" she yelled and ran up the stairs.

M'Shara turned and stood in front of Elena halting her before she could gain any more speed. "Stop, Elena," she commanded.

Elena was confused. "Mother, you would

have us stand idly by and listen to these lies about my blood?"

M'Shara placed her hands on her daughter's shoulders. "It is true. Kane is your father." She exhaled when she said those words; they had been pent up for too long.

Elena was stunned. She couldn't speak. She backed away down the stairs and took off in a flash. Decio followed. The lord and empress stood from their thrones and watched as M'Shara turned and approached them.

LaVius slid his hand under his wife's chin and ushered her near for a tender kiss. "You did what had to be done. I will leave you two alone." He then turned and nodded good evening to M'Shara and slipped away.

The two old friends stood silently staring at each other. Neither knew where to begin. Their secrets were out—but only one in its entirety. Finally, M'Shara broke the silence. "Domnina, you told her about Kane—"

"Yes. But isn't it for the best? I believe, M'Shara that this night was inevitable, and that Elena is old enough and strong enough to handle the truth about my brother. I think the more probing question is—are you?"

M'Shara knew what her friend meant by this. She had loved Kane for what seemed like an eternity, but he had a dark side. He was quick to enrage. Deep inside him was a ferocious beast that once unleashed could be deadly to anyone and anything in his path. Part of him loathed that side of himself. He wanted to marry M'Shara, but knew the danger was too great. Although he had never harmed her, he chose to leave before she gave birth to their child. He would not risk the safety of either one of them. Kane made M'Shara swear to never tell their daughter about him. He wouldn't have her know what a beast he was.

On the night of Elena's birth, Domnina and two nursemaids were in attendance. When the empress felt her brother near, she secretly slipped out of M'Shara's cottage in her cloak and hood. She peered into the darkness and saw her brother's glowing eyes in the dark woods. He then took off. He had just seen the birth of his child from the window, but wouldn't come nearer. He was overcome with sorrow because he couldn't be with them, and had run away into the night. Domnina told M'Shara of this. The two women vowed to share the secret together, knowing the far-off day would come that Elena would have to be told the truth.

The empress could still see affection and a sense of loss in M'Shara's eyes as they spoke of Kane. "M'Shara? You still love him, don't you?"

M'Shara inhaled sharply. "Of course not."

The empress raised her head in disbelief. "I see. Then you will not be happy to see him?"

M'Shara was stammered by that remark. "See him? When?"

The empress's lips curved into a satiated smile. "Tonight."

M'Shara swallowed hard and lost her breath. She had not seen Kane in nearly thirty years. In their immortal lives it was not long, but to her it seemed like an eternity. Her voice was shaky. "Tonight?" she echoed.

"Yes, my dear friend. I have sent for him. In fact, he is not far. You will be staying, won't you?"

"No, I mean—I think it better if I—well—" "If you what?" said a deep voice behind her.

His words pulsed in her veins. The sound of him made her body instantly shudder. He slid his strong hand onto her shoulder and turned her around. It was Kane. M'Shara fainted into his arms.

The empress simply smiled. "Welcome home brother."

CHAPTER SIX

K ane lifted M'Shara into his arms and carried her. He followed his sister along the stone veranda and into the great hall. Once there, the empress stopped a servant and requested he summon LaVius. Kane and Empress Domnina then took M'Shara down the hall to the evening room at the back of the castle. It had waterfalls on either side of the room, and faced the outdoors openly via a balcony which spanned the entire width of the room.

It was incredibly serene. Domnina walked out to the balcony and Kane gently laid M'Shara on the divan. He then went to join his sister on the terrace.

"It is wonderful to see you brother," she said in a caring tone rarely heard by anyone.

His scalp was smooth, his jaw defined. He was very tall, strong and handsome. Domnina was proud of her younger brother and he was of her. He inhaled deeply and turned his eyes to the moonlit landscape. "I'm glad to see you as well, Domnina, but it is a bittersweet return."

Domnina knew of what he spoke. "Let us not dwell in the past," she said. "You have gained control over your emotions—better than anyone else with the affliction ever has."

He glowered at her. "It is not an affliction."

She put her hand on his arm to calm him. "I know that, Kane. I'm sorry. You should be proud of having such control, but it is not something to be ashamed of either. You should be proud of your heritage. It's in your blood—in our blood."

He calmed down a little. He knew she spoke the truth. The agramon strain was in their bloodline, but it has only rarely ever become active. In Kane, it was not only active, but was the most potent form of the venomous blood, and by far the most dangerous. Even so, he knew that his sister would prefer it if he embraced that uniquely dark side of himself.

"Domnina, I know you want what is best for me, but I am concerned for M'Shara and for—my daughter." It was difficult for him to say those words, 'my daughter.' He'd only whispered them. For so many years he forced himself to stay out of her life. Learning to control his anger had been a far easier task.

Suddenly, LaVius appeared. "You've come home, Kane. Are you back for good?"

Kane turned to see his lovely M'Shara lying on the divan silently. He'd longed for her, ached for her every moment since he left. Secretly, over the years, he would come close at times just to catch a glimpse of her and of Elena, and then he would slip away unnoticed.

He answered LaVius in a solemn tone. "I haven't decided."

The empress and LaVius secretly looked at each other knowingly. Kane's eyes were fixed on M'Shara.

"Kane," LaVius interjected, "Your eternity can unfold however you'd like. Alone is but one option."

Kane fully understood the meaning of those words, and they'd caught him by surprise. LaVius took his wife by the hand and the two slipped away into the dark shadows of the castle.

Kane gingerly neared M'Shara. He knelt down beside her and listened carefully to her breathing. He counted each breath. He gazed over her exquisite sable skin that he'd longed to touch, and the delicate features of her face that he'd memorized long ago. His breath began to quicken, he nearly lost control of his emotions, but held strong. He boldly moved his strong hand to her face and tenderly stroked her cheek with his fingertips. Her eyes slowly fluttered open. He gasped at the loveliness of those warm, deep, brown eyes that he'd yearned to see. The eyes that always made him feel so loved and so at peace.

Those eyes now stared at him with astonishment. M'Shara had not only missed Kane desperately, but craved him. She's tried for so long to push him out of her mind, yet here he was. She felt it must be a dream. She uncontrollably uttered the words, "Are you really here?"

He smiled and lowered his mouth to her. They shared a kiss so passionate, so incredibly overdue; it was a kiss that would make up for all of the countless days and years apart. Their love was unremitting. It was as if not a single moment had passed and they had never been parted.

LaVius and Domnina stood in the pitch darkness on the balcony of their bed chamber. "They say my brother is a fearsome creature that no man can tame," Domnina recalled.

"I agree," LaVius answered. "But they made no mention of a woman."

CHAPTER Seven

"Elena, stop! We've run far enough. Stop and talk to me." Decio was worried about her. It pained his heart to know that she was hurting.

Elena stopped running in the middle of a valley. The moon shone brightly right above them. They'd run a great distance from the castle. She dropped to the grass and sobbed. Decio rushed to her side. "My dear, please speak to me. Tell me what is so wrong?"

She stopped crying as she felt a sudden calmness with Decio nearby. "Decio, this isn't the way it was supposed to be."

"Things rarely are," he replied.

"But Domnina… and then her brother… it can't be." Elena gripped her hair with her hands. "It isn't possible!" she screamed.

"Elena, it's all so clear now. We both knew her command made no sense, and now to find out it was to protect us… to protect you, her niece."

"Don't say that word." Elena couldn't absorb all of this, as much as she tried.

"Listen," Decio continued. "We must think this through. Her rules were only to shield us. And now that we know about the prophecy, maybe we can find a way to stop it."

Elena's whirling mind began to calm down. "You still want to be with me after all you heard?"

Decio was stunned. "Of course! I've wanted nothing else for my entire life. We will be married, and nothing can stop us now."

"But what about the prophecy?" Elena questioned.

Decio took her by the hand. "We know the truth now, and nothing could ever make me hurt you. We can do this. All we have to do is make it past the wedding night."

"And that talk about my father, Kane. What about him? I've heard stories of the son of Lucifer. He is supposed to be a terrifying beast. It isn't possible. My mother would never love someone like that. It just can't be true."

Elena was overwhelmed with query. Decio pulled her close. "Maybe things are not as plain as they would seem, Elena."

Elena lifted her eyes to his. "What do you mean?"

"I mean that you cannot judge a person by the stories you hear about them, or by the roles they must play in effort to keep order in our world."

Elena knew that he spoke of Kane and also of Lord LaVius and Domnina. She sat quietly and listened to him as he tenderly wiped the tears from her eyes.

"We do not know what is in the hearts of others. If your mother loved Kane once, there must be a reason."

Elena lowered her eyes again. Decio's words seemed wise. She had a lot more to consider than she'd thought, but she was still overwhelmed.

"Do not be troubled, my love," said Decio. "We will sort this out, together."

CHAPTER EIGHT

Elena and Decio lay on the grass in that valley and slept until dawn. As the sun rose, she began to feel the pangs of hunger. Although she had trained herself to mostly feast on the nectar from plants in lieu of blood, the stresses of being home had made her weary; she felt she needed blood. As she lay there on the cool grass, trying to curb the feeling of hunger she was distracted by the strikingly handsome features of her husband-to-be as he slept. She smiled. Her heart was warmed by his presence.

For a moment everything seemed perfect.

But she was snatched back to reality when she recalled the prophecy. On the wedding night, Decio would destroy her? Elena knew it wasn't possible, but the thought made her sick with worry. Decio felt her anxiety and immediately awoke.

Decio felt her anxiety and immediately awoke.

"Elena, what is it? Is something the matter?" he asked.

His voice soothed her. Every word he breathed seemed to dance gracefully into her heart. She smiled. "Nothing, Decio. Nothing we can't get through."

They stood together and held hands. He grinned handsomely. "Then shall we eat?"

"Yes, let's," she agreed. And they went off to hunt together.

While Decio searched for a grisly-looking animal or two, Elena tried to curb her bloodlust by snacking on honeysuckle and hibiscus. She remembered that her mother loved hibiscus tea. She stuffed some of the petals into her pouch. Decio soon sneaked up on Elena which startled her into a fit of hilarity. She then ran so that he would chase her through the flowers and trees. They laughed and had the time of their lives. Finally, Decio twirled her around and they began to dance.

"There is no music, Decio," Elena laughed.

"But you're wrong, Elena," he stated. "Your smile fills my soul with an everlasting song." He then twirled her around once more and shouted toward the sky, "I cannot wait to marry you!"

CHAPTER Nine

Empress Domnina, dressed in a black leather riding suit, prepared to ride her beloved horse, Oblivion. Oblivion was a hot-blooded Barb: onyx in color, tall, muscular, and fierce. Her size, speed, and strength were what the empress revered, and were only equaled by one other horse in the land: Oblivion's mate, Phenom, which belonged to Lord LaVius. Both horses had a malevolent temperament, their breaths were a searing steam, their eyes black pools of aggression. They yielded to no one but the lord and empress.

As the empress stood outside the stable next to Oblivion and tightened the girth on her saddle, someone slipped from behind and placed a breathtaking bouquet of scarlet Bomarea flowers in front of her. She took them and smiled. She didn't turn to see his face, but the intoxicating musk of him filled her senses with familiarity. Her husband's hair draped over her shoulder as he bent and sweetly kissed her on the neck. She turned to him. "You're supposed to be a fearsome lord," she reminded when she turned around.

"But the sheer sight of you brings me such light that I forget myself," he grinned.

She shook her head. He often made her forget herself as well. LaVius helped her onto the horse. She stared slyly into his eyes while she pulled her gloves on. "Don't you be good while I'm gone, or you'll have to answer to me," she teased.

"Don't worry my dear. When you're not around, I promise, I can be a real beast."

"Good." She winked at him with a smile and tucked the flowers neatly into the swell of the saddle.

LaVius then leaned on the horse. "Speaking of keeping true to your sinister side—what about that little lie you told Elena in order to protect her mother?"

She tightened her lips. "Well, I suppose we're both going soft now, aren't we?" she pointed out.

"I'm sure it will pass."

"Good."

He smacked the back of the horse and bellowed, "Yah!" and the horse took off like a thunderbolt.

CHAPTER Ten

M'Shara and Kane spent the entire night talking and basking in each other's presence. They had a great deal to catch up on, much healing to do, and they'd come a long way. Kane never left her side for a moment that entire night. Now that it was morning, they walked along the grounds together, taking in the sight of the wonderful gardens, sculptures, and fountains. M'Shara held firmly onto Kane's hand, never wanting to let go.

"M'Shara, Elena has grown into a sophisticated and independent being. But the vampirism, I wish I'd been able to stop it."

"Kane, it has been a decade since that happened," M'Shara stated.

Kane stopped walking and turned to her. "I know. I was there. I killed the beast that infected our daughter."

M'Shara was confounded. Kane had told her during their earlier talk that he'd secretly kept an eye on them, but she didn't know just how much, until now.

Kane continued. "I was nearby in the woods, and sensed something was dreadfully wrong with Elena. My blood began to boil, my heart to pound. I ran instinctively to where I knew she was, and when I found her, it was too late. The creature was upon her. She was unconscious and never saw me take after the beast. My rage was more furious than at any time in my life. After a few moments my prey ceased to exist." Kane swallowed hard.

M'Shara didn't know what to say. All of these long years Kane had suffered alone.

He looked into her eyes and saw her anguish. "What is wrong?" he asked.

"Kane, you had no one to comfort you. No

one to turn to."

He stroked her hair to soothe her. "I had my sister at times. I felt foolish and refused to run to her with my problems, but whenever I would stay away too long, she would seek me out. She would search for me and make sure I was all right. Even at my most loathsome, Domnina has always embraced me. She has always been there for me. For that I am grateful. But I still felt hollow, alone. Without you I have never been whole.

"Those days are over, Kane," M'Shara sobbed. "I will hold you in my arms forever. You will never feel alone again."

The two embraced firmly and just breathed each other. Their souls were finally at peace. They would never part again.

Lord LaVius strolled back to the castle from the stables. As he approached, one of his messengers came running toward him, nearly stumbling over his own feet. The boy, out of breath and very bewildered, immediately bowed to his majesty and held up a letter. "This just came for you, Lord," the child said nervously, rushing to kneel.

LaVius took the letter. "Stand up, boy." The

letter bore the mark of Soren, Governor of the Realm of Blithe. It read:

Your Majesty, Emperor LaVius

A matter of terrific urgency is at hand. A creature long thought dormant has attacked and virtually obliterated the village of Amity. Fortunately, no one bitten has survived. They are the agramon. We are not certain of their numbers, however believe there are six. They make way to the Realm of Shadows.

LaVius sent a falcon to warn the empress. The falcons could communicate telepathically and Domnina would immediately be made aware of the scope of the situation. The falcon, Anistar, could reach her faster than any rider. LaVius stayed behind to summon his guard and send them to scour the plains in search of the beasts. Once he did so, he immediately went to speak with Kane.

"Kane, we must speak at once," LaVius informed him. When the two men's eyes met, Kane knew it was serious, and that LaVius was actually asking him if M'Shara should hear what he was about to say.

Kane silently nodded to LaVius that it was all right to speak plainly in front of M'Shara. "What is it, LaVius?"

LaVius continued hesitantly. "Agramon," he said firmly.

Kane was staggered. "Agramon? How? Where?"

M'Shara gripped Kane's arm tightly. She was shocked and alarmed by this news.

"They left Amity last night. They head this way," LaVius answered.

Kane's breath began to quicken. "That is less than a hundred miles from our closest border."

"Yes. And they're quick, and do not sleep when they are on the hunt. It won't be long until they reach these lands."

LaVius and Kane stared into each other's eyes; words were not needed. They both knew what this meant, and so did M'Shara. LaVius's guard combined could easily defend the land against these creatures, but they would have to find them first—and all of them. These creatures were clever, unyielding, and malicious. They would prey on any living thing in their sights.

Once bitten by one of the creatures, any human would wish for death, as he would inevitably transform into the great beast, a process that was arduous and brutally painful. A vampire bitten by one of these beasts would also be overcome with the fiercest form of blood lust. The vampire's rage and thirst would be uncontrollable, even to himself. But this wasn't the only concern. The most prevalent concern was that Kane was an agramon. He'd learn restraint, but agramon are connected to one another. With other agramon near, Kane's inner rage might be cajoled into a form too great to contain. LaVius, Kane, and M'Shara all knew this.

CHAPTER ELEVEN

D omnina rode furiously across the plains
along the outer edge of the forest. All at
once, she was struck by a feeling of unease.
Something was amiss in the land of shadows,
something unexpected. Next, she was forewarned
of the presence of a magical being when her
inferno ruby began to seethe. She was on full
alert. All of her senses heightened.

As she rode Oblivion, maintaining top speed,
she never turned her head, but her eyes and other
senses scanned the area. Anistar soared through
the air and down alongside her. He soared past

her and she heard his message loud and clear. He soon disappeared. The empress now knew of the coming agramon, and because of her previous unease, was concerned that one of them might have already arrived. She didn't feel that the burning of her ring was from the nearness of Anistar alone.

Suddenly, the empress saw what she was expecting to see. Ahead of her, at a distance, an agramon tore out of the forest. He was a giant— tall and exceedingly muscular. He was bald, his skin was tight and his fists were clenched as he sprinted toward her.

Empress Domnina was no stranger to such beasts; she had dealt with her brother and many more. She leapt from the speeding horse and dashed toward the monster.

He let out a thunderous roar and she gritted her teeth as she ran. As they neared one another at top speed, Domnina snatched a large hunting blade from her boot. He lunged for her and she hurdled up and over his shoulder, slicing him across the neck as she went. He howled and bled profusely, but was still very much alive. Domnina knew full well it would take much more to get him down.

From his back, she gouged him again between the shoulder blades. The fell beast reached back and grabbed her. He flung her thirty feet across the ground. He growled hungrily and started toward her. He wasn't used to a fight from anyone, but was fueled by his rage. Domnina glowered and took a sprinting stance. Smoke surged from his throat when he roared.

They lunged at one another again and he knocked her spinning across the field once more, this time slicing her across the ribs with his nails. She bled on the grass, the leather of her top torn and bloody, but she had no time or desire for pain.

The empress climbed to her knees and then to her feet. She was weakened, but furious. "Come here, you monotonous filth!" she screamed at him. "Is that all you've got?"

The agramon started toward her, thirsty for blood. His sharp teeth in full view as he ran, he intended this to be the last pursuit. He would tear her to shreds and feast on her broken body.

Domnina could barely stand but was ready for him. Instantly, the monster pounced. He forced

Domnina to the ground and towered above her. As she was about to stab him with her blade, he took her side into his mouth and sunk his teeth in firmly—but before he could tear the meat away, M'Shara appeared on the plains next to her horse. She stood firmly, the wind struggling with her cloak, and screamed "Halt, beast!"

The monster released his hold on the empress and rose up to see M'Shara. She then thrust her hands forward and a great force of purple and green light flooded the field. It stunned all movement including that of the agramon.

With the creature frozen for a time, Domnina stood tall, and lunged her blade directly into the heart of the monster. When he came to, he bellowed a horrific yell toward the sky and crashed onto his back dying slowly, but surely.

Domnina stood over him out of breath and cocked her head toward her approaching comrade. "Thanks, friend," she uttered.

M'Shara's lips curved into a grin. "I owed you one."

Oblivion returned to the empress and wearily she climbed onto the horse's back.

"You are in no condition to ride," M'Shara

informed her.

Domnina just smirked. "It takes more than a raging monster to get me down," she answered.

"Nonetheless," M'Shara scoffed. "We'll ride slowly."

Domnina leaned forward on the saddle and whispered to her Oblivion. Then, while she held her bloody ribs, the women conversed on the journey back to the citadel.

"Domnina—" M'Shara began. "Why did you do it?"

"Why did I do what?" the empress asked cautiously.

"You lied to Elena and Decio about the prophecy," her friend explained.

The empress had known it would only be a matter of time before M'Shara spoke of this. She remained silent.

M'Shara continued. "We both know full-well that the portents say I will be the one to kill Decio."

The weakened empress shook her head. "Elena is my brother's daughter, and she's suffered enough. She already resents me. You are all she's ever had."

M'Shara's heart was warmed. Domnina never showed much compassion. "Empress, you amaze me. That is the most selfless act of giving. You aren't as dark as you would have people believe."

Domnina's exhausted eyes grew wide. "Nonsense," she insisted.

M'Shara simply smiled to herself.

Chapter Twelve

" The full moon is just three nights from now,"
Decio whispered.

The two had ventured to M'Shara's home and
stood outside. Elena had relaxed and was more
than ready to see her mother again. She wanted to
apologize for the outburst at the castle and for
running away. "Yes, Decio," Elena replied with a
joyous grin. "Three nights, and you shall be mine
forever."

"I am already yours forever," he corrected and
gave her a peck on the cheek.

She laughed merrily and went up to M'Shara's

door. Dusk had fallen, and the woods were misty and dark. The cottage was quiet. Elena sensed her mother was not at home. She couldn't feel her familiar energy. The door creaked as she opened it, and they went inside. Elena wasn't paying close attention or her senses would have felt the same thing Decio's had. He felt they were not alone. Elena took the hibiscus petals from her pouch and set them on the wooden counter. Decio scanned the room and halted his eyes on a figure sitting in the shadows. He knew who it was. Just at that moment, Elena lighted a lantern which illuminated the room and the figure's face. She was caught off guard and screamed.

The tall figure stood from M'Shara's chair and slowly approached Elena. She took her battle stance preparing for attack. Decio stood calmly and lit a second lantern. The figure held up his hands as he came into full lighted view. "Elena, please don't be afraid. I would never hurt you," he pleaded. He'd never spoken to his daughter before, never been close enough for her to see him.

"Who are you?!" she demanded.

"I am your father," said Kane with emotion in

his voice.

He took another step forward and she gasped for breath. When he'd said those words, she knew it was true. "My father," she mouthed.

"Yes, Elena. Please let me look at you."

"Stay back!" she shouted. She began to sob. "I don't have a father. Stay back..." she spoke a little weaker this time and with less feeling.

He grabbed her and she let him. He began to weep. "I have longed for this moment your entire life," he said. "I never want to let go."

She could barely speak through her tears. She wept into his chest, her fists trying vainly to pound him. She wanted to fight him, but couldn't. She too had longed for this moment. Her mind was finally grasping that it was true. This man was her father. Part of her always knew he was near and would return to her life, but she never allowed herself to believe it. "Why haven't you been in my life?" she asked. "Why?"

Kane, Decio, and Elena had a long and rich conversation. Kane admitted to his daughter, however reluctantly, what was in his blood: his true reason for staying away. But he hadn't truly been away. He had kept watch over her and over

M'Shara in secret. He had seen Elena grow up and had seen M'Shara turn down other suitors. He now felt complete. For the first time in years, he could begin to live and would never have to hide again.

"There is more," Kane warned. "There are agramon on the loose. They have made way to this realm. The black guard is on the hunt for them, but I came here to warn you. You must come to the castle with me. You will be safe there."

"Father," Elena blurted before she realized what she'd said. She'd never said that to anyone before.

"Yes, daughter," said Kane.

"We plan to live in Decio's home at the edge of Redway. We go there tonight. We will be safe."

"Elena, you must listen to me. The black citadel is a fortress. There is no safer place. You cannot understand the ferocity of these beasts the way I do. Please see reason."

Decio took Elena's hand. "Your father is right. We must go. I wish to keep you as safe as possible. I cannot imagine a safer place than the palace of the Lord LaVius. Can you?"

Elena gritted her teeth. She agreed with both of them, but didn't like to be told what to do. "Fine, but I go of my own free will."

Kane laughed joyfully. "Your mother would have said those exact words."

CHAPTER THIRTEEN

Night had closed in on the realm as Domnina and M'Shara rode through the black gates. Domnina had taken a longer route when she'd left, but M'Shara led them back using the shortest path possible.

LaVius had felt the hearts of the women nearing and his connection to Domnina's warned him that something wasn't right. He burst open the castle doors and ran out to meet them. He wore his black riding pants and boots and a loosely tucked black tunic as he'd been preparing to ride out to meet his guard. He saw his wife slumped forward on the mare. "What is this?" he shouted.

"Agramon," said M'Shara.

She then dismounted and the stablemen quickly came to take the horses away. It wouldn't be an easy task, so Domnina, albeit frail and fading, spoke to Oblivion, telling the animal to calmly go.

LaVius slipped his wife off of the horse and carried her bloody frame. "I don't need you to carry..." she began, but was too weak to finish. She tried to slide her arms around his neck, but her strength waned and they simply dropped.

LaVius and M'Shara had never seen the empress in such a state. She was, after all, immortal just as they were. As LaVius hurried to their bed chamber, his monstrous voice bellowed through the walls of the castle. He demanded every attendant prepare to assist them without delay. M'Shara followed quickly.

When they arrived in the chambers, four nursemaids were already there. LaVius expected no less. They'd prepared a clean linen chemise, bandages, and a cauldron of water was warming over the fire. One of them threw back the coverings and LaVius laid his wife onto the bed gently. He sat next to her and examined her wounds. "An agramon did this?" he wondered aloud.

He tore the rest of the leather from her side and saw just how severe the wound was. He now knew the reason for her weakness, as did she.

Domnina and her brother were of kimaris blood, as was LaVius. This numinous blood was powerful, and Kane learned over time that it helped him control his rage. But the siblings were also of agramon blood; the volatile characteristics of which were not active in Domnina, but gave her brother unspeakable strength and a furious temperament. It also caused him to produce a deadly venom that is even more potent at the peak of his rage.

The beast that attacked Domnina was a subspecies of agramon. LaVius knew this because Domnina's wound was turning black; a conclusive sign of their fetid venom. This species was thought by many in the outer realms to be extinct. But those in the dark lands knew better. These agramon had been bred for destruction.

The venom of the subspecies can be fatal to

the kimaris. With a wound such as Domnina's,
death is likely inescapable.

Domnina was pale. She opened her eyes and
stared deeply into her husband's. When their eyes
met, she could feel no pain, no despair, only
devotion. "I will be fine, my dear LaVius. Go. Go
and kill the beasts."

He leaned over and kissed her forehead hard.
His hand gripped the back of her hair and his eyes
closed tightly as he deeply inhaled. He couldn't
bear to see her injured like this; frail, weakened.
Every one of the remaining beasts would pay. He
motioned for the nursemaids to tend her. He and
M'Shara stepped out into the hallway to speak. He
explained of the reason for Domnina's condition,
and M'Shara assured him the agramon that did
this was in fact dead. He turned quickly to leave.
M'Shara grabbed his arm.

"Lord LaVius—what of Kane?"

"He went to find your daughter," he said.
Then he left, hurrying down the stairs and out of
her sight.

M'Shara gasped and covered her mouth with
her hand. Kane and Elena. She was nervous about
their meeting, but felt deep inside that it was the

right time. She was also nervous about Kane, Elena, and Decio alone in the forest. She didn't know how far they might be and whether they were safe. She'd been distracted before, concerned about Domnina. But now, as she allowed her mind to open and explore, her clairvoyance told her that Kane and Elena were together, and her heart told her that together they would be just fine.

As LaVius mounted Phenom, fire burned in his eyes. A rage he had not recently felt was brewing inside of him. Two members of his guard rode up beside him. "My lord, what is the battle plan?"

LaVius's eyes darkened and turned slowly to the man; his voice was like thunder, "Hell will be raised tonight." And they sped off into the darkness.

Chapter Fourteen

M'Shara watched over her friend as she
winced and moaned in her sleep. She
wished there was more she could do, but there
seemed to be nothing. Finally, when all was quiet,
M'Shara slipped a coral dish from the poplar
chest next to the door then flitted away to the
evening room where she could be alone.

M'Shara took the dish and slid it into a
waterfall until it was filled. She then sat in silence
at a table and relaxed into a meditative state. She
slowly glided her hands about the air above the
bowl and an image began to appear. It was

night… Elena's wedding, and the full moon was high. She and Decio looked happy. But M'Shara could see no one else. She tried, but could not get a clear view of the others. *Is Kane there? Am I? What about LaVius or Domnina? Does she make it through this illness?* She pondered all of these questions silently. She tried hard to see a glimmer of someone else's face—anyone's, a face that might give her insight into what will happen. Alas, she'd probably tried too hard. She decided she was much too close to the situation to get a clear vision. Her mind was biased. M'Shara was very upset by this. She felt helpless. She slammed her fists onto the table. "Damn!" she yelled.

"Mother! What's going on?" Elena blurted as she, Decio, and Kane entered the room.

M'Shara flew from her chair. "Oh, Elena! You are here! I'm so thankful!"

The two embraced, catching up for not only the last few nights, but for all of the lost time between them. She then took Decio's hand and smiled at him. She was grateful that he never left her daughter's side, and knew he would be a fierce protector. She just hoped in some way that this prophecy would not come to pass.

She then turned to Kane. As her eyes met his, she reached up and placed her hands gently on either side of his face. Her eyes told him how incredibly jubilant she was that he had found their daughter, and that the two had made peace, but also that she had pressing news he needed to hear.

"I am filled with joy that my family is all together," she cried. "But Kane—it's about Domnina—"

Kane felt a sudden uneasiness about him. He knew something wasn't right in the castle when they first arrived. "Where is she?" he boomed.

"In her chambers," said M'Shara. "Kane—it was an agramon."

Kane flew out of sight in an instant. He raced immediately to his sister's side. M'Shara stayed with her daughter and Decio and filled them in on the day's events.

Kane entered the room and saw his sister lying on the bed. She was sleeping. She wore a plain white gown and an eiderdown quilt was pulled up to her waist. Her long dark hair was loosely strewn about the pillows; her face, lips, and hands had lost most of their color. He saw the bloody rags that one of the women had taken from her and put in a basin. He knelt next to the bed and held Domnina's hand into the both of his. "How can this be?" he groaned, both sadly and angrily. "How!" he yelled. His breaths became deep and forceful. As his chest began to rise and lower intensely, a low growl began to emanate from within him.

The two nursemaids that stood by froze with fear. Kane's eyes were becoming red; his jaw began to clench and he looked as if he were fighting something back—something dreadful. He quickly dropped Domnina's hand. Kane began to shudder and it shook the floor.

The nursemaids ran swiftly for their lives.

CHAPTER FIFTEEN

D ecio stood leaning on the massive arched entryway, his arms crossed. He had been listening to Elena and her mother converse over serious matters, but something suddenly distracted him. He was used to the scent of other magical beings; the realm was full of them, and he usually could have cared less. But this was the intoxicating aroma of ordinary human blood. His brow lowered; his taste buds tingled.

He hadn't prepared himself for this. When Decio contemplated staying at the black palace, he never considered mortals would be nearby. A few had been at the solstice ball, but this—this had caught him off guard. He clenched his eyes closed and tried to control the urgency he felt inside. He could feel them nearing—there were two of them. They approached quickly from behind him. He could hear their blood pumping hard and fast in his ears; they were running. Like a flash he turned and had them both by the throats. He now stood in the archway holding them. They were the nursemaids.

Elena had better control over her hunger than Decio. She and M'Shara rushed over to stop him. With Elena's incredible speed she reached him in an instant. "Decio—no!"

He gritted his teeth and stared into the eyes of each lady. Elena tried to stand between Decio and the two women. She forced her strong hand into his chest to stop him. "Decio, it's all right. Let them go."

The two women had been running from the sight of Kane, but unknowingly ran right into the hands of further danger. M'Shara stood still for a moment. She was more than a little curious as to why the two nursemaids had left Domnina's side and had run so hastily into this situation. She knew something was terribly wrong and ran to Kane and Domnina.

Elena's words began to quell Decio's intensity. He released the women and they collapsed to the floor gasping for any bit of air. Elena was fighting back her own craving for the blood; and the women, upon realizing their peril, found the strength to take off running once more.

Decio dashed into the other direction and Elena followed him into the night. Decio was no longer comfortable staying there. He didn't want to dishonor Lord LaVius nor any of Elena's family by butchering their servants. Elena understood, but was reminded of the reasons Decio agreed with her father that they should stay in the castle in the first place. The forest was too risky right now. However, by the time she stopped him from running; they were eleven leagues away.

Upstairs at the castle, M'Shara had reached Domnina's side. Her friend was still quiescent; Kane was nowhere in sight. In a corner of the room M'Shara saw a stone table crushed into rubble. Lying with it was the bowl, now broken and devoid of water, and the bloody rags. M'Shara turned her eyes to the balcony; the drapes danced and twirled in the wind. She stepped slowly to them and parted them wide. There, Kane stood as she'd hoped. His hands firmly gripped the stone wall. His shirt, which was still tucked, but now lay down torn into shreds, left his upper body exposed. M'Shara could see the great tension in his muscles as he heavily breathed and she knew what had almost happened. She slowly approached Kane and gingerly placed her hand on his shoulder to comfort him. "Kane, are you all right?" she whispered.

He forcibly swallowed and turned toward M'Shara. They gazed at each other. His eyes began to cool from smoldering red to the tranquil hue that always reminded M'Shara of the evening sea. As his intensity subsided, he cupped her cheek with his hand. "I'm sorry..." he began.

M'Shara hushed him gently. "Kane, don't. Don't worry about what you almost did—because you didn't. Everything is all right. And I love you. Don't apologize." She smiled at him warmly.

"I'm not apologizing for that, my love," he said tenderly; his look beginning to change. "I'm apologizing for leaving." He kissed her forehead softly then declared, "I've got killing to do." With that, Kane left M'Shara's sight in an instant, a murderous storm in his eyes.

CHAPTER SIXTEEN

The imperial guard, led by their master, rode across the dark plains toward the far reaches of the realm, searching for the agramon. Kane was separately on the hunt. His rage was in check, but he wanted it so. He kept hold of his anger that it may be unleashed when the time was right. As far as Kane and LaVius were concerned, these beasts had done more than cross into the wrong realm—they were the reason Domnina lay dying. More than blood would be shed this night.

The two young vampires were far from the safety

of the black palace where the remaining members of the guard kept watch. Decio, who'd run off most of his steam, sat with his bride-to-be atop a giant spruce gazing at the stars.

"Your mother and father will worry," Decio realized. "You shouldn't have followed me."

Elena was aghast. "I shouldn't have followed you?"

"I couldn't stay there, but you could have. You would be much safer."

"Decio, first, I am fully able to handle myself in the wilderness. And second, I have no care of the dangers; I would follow you to the end of the universe."

Decio gazed across the blackness of the plains. "I know," he said sadly. "And you would risk your own life to do it."

"Yes," she replied.

"You mustn't. You must go back," Decio insisted.

Elena refused. "I will not leave you. Don't breathe those words again!"

"Elena, you—" Suddenly something caught Decio's eye. He swiftly and quietly rose to his feet on the branch and peered into the dark at

something that moved. About a hundred yards
from them something barreled through the brush,
something enormous, something that moved with
purpose—something that wasn't alone.

M'Shara paced back and forth on the balcony
outside Domnina's chambers. She was incensed at
being unable to figure a cure for her friend's
condition. "I know there is a spell—a tincture—
something!" she cried out. She stomped across
the stone terrace thinking hard and deep. She then
paused for a moment and parted the curtains. She
looked into the room where Domnina laid. Her
friend was still; she seemed hard as stone. She was
immortal, yet now so distant from the world; she
was near death. M'Shara was overwhelmed with
emotion as well as query. She knew there was
something she could do, but what?

M'Shara's eyes spanned the room and finally
rested on the table that Kane had obliterated. She
thought of his incalculable strength. She asked
herself why Domnina couldn't be that strong
right now; if only for a few moments. Then she
saw the bloody rags that once wrapped her friend,
and she wished Domnina's blood was more like

Kane's tonight. If she were more like her brother, then she wouldn't be in this state. *She would be walking among us*, M'Shara thought. "And she would probably be out there fighting alongside her husband and Kane," she murmured.

M'Shara grew angry at this travesty. She ground her teeth and turned to the stone rail of the balcony. She peered out at the dark landscape almost giving up hope at ever finding a cure. She hung her head low—then shot it back up in an instant. She had a revelation. "That's it!" M'Shara screamed. She ran to Domnina's side gleefully, and so quickly that she almost tangled her feet in the length of her cloak. "Domnina! Domnina!" she cried cheerfully. "In all your wicked malevolence you lie there quietly—but I know you can hear me!" M'Shara laughed and put one hand to her heart and clasped Domnina's hand with the other. "I know how to help you, friend! But I must find Kane! I shall return!"

LaVius slowed Phenom to a halt. The horse groaned ferociously. "Quiet boy," LaVius warned. "I feel them too."

Two men of the guard were with LaVius and

took notice of his actions. They too stopped and prepared for the coming ambush. "It is time," LaVius grinned evilly. "They don't know what's waiting for them. Let them come. I will thoroughly enjoy this slaughter."

The three men drew their swords, but first, LaVius dismounted. All at once three agramon jumped from the trees and the battle began. LaVius's eyes became blood red with fury. He wielded his sword, intent on annihilation. The first agramon was the largest, at least ten feet, and its shoulders were four wide. The monster growled and thrashed its massive arms at LaVius. Its teeth were made for tearing; its body sculpted into an immense muscular fighting machine. But LaVius would show him who was master of this domain.

LaVius lunged at the creature, bludgeoning its belly with the two-handed blade. He then ripped it out with all his force through the monster's side. The agramon wailed angrily, but remained standing. LaVius's hair whipped around as he leapt up using the beast's leg for leverage. In an instant, he caught its throat with the bend of his arm and twisted the muscular neck until it was no longer of use. The beast fell to the ground and LaVius jumped over it and toward the next one. The two guards were in need of assistance.

Elena stood up and next to Decio on the large tree limb. "What is it?" she whispered.

"Agramon—" said Decio, "two of them."

The two beasts crossed the field and neared the tree where Decio and Elena stood.

"Wait here," Decio instructed his wife-to-be.

Her brows turned in defiantly. "Like hell," she answered, and jumped down onto the back of one of the agramon.

Decio shook his head and followed suit.

CHAPTER Seventeen

Elena, now on the back of one of the Lagramon, tried to reach around and claw at his eyes. It was a bold effort but the beast snatched her from its back and flung her onto the ground, much like the empress had been thrown earlier. Her arm twisted, and her vampire blood began to boil. Her own animal instinct took over and she ran toward the monster. Then, like flashes of light, she dodged his thrashes. She bobbed and weaved in and out of his reach, slicing him with her razor-sharp nails. She was much too fast for him, but this would not kill him.

The second agramon was much larger and had black hair that surged from the top of his skull down to his back. The beast's eyes glowed white; its teeth were red with blood. The beast had been moving toward Decio, but Elena caught his attention. It noticed how fast she was and thought his cohort foolish for letting her play this game. He would remind him that his job was to tear her apart. He ran past Decio and barreled into the other agramon, sparking a brawl between the two that left Decio and Elena thunderstruck. The rage between the two monsters seemed to escalate and their roars echoed throughout the land.

"Decio, now is our chance to get away. They are distracted." She knew that their vampire speed would be impossible for the agramon to contend with.

However, Decio's eyes had grown dark. "You go. I will stay and fight."

Elena grabbed hold of Decio's arm. "Decio, you can't!" she whispered loudly.

"I must. We are far from the citadel and no one knows they are here. If I can hold them, you can go back and send assistance."

Before Decio could go on, the two agramon refocused their fury—both of them on him. The first one knelt on all fours and stared the male vampire down as if he were prey; its wounds from Elena's claws were dripping. The larger one raised his head menacingly and sniffed the air. It was as if there was a familiar scent on the wind. He looked about cautiously, but returned his white eyes to Decio whose own eyes were red and fixed upon him. The two agramon slowly made their steps toward Decio and showed the gnarly teeth that they planned to sink into his tough pale skin.

Elena suddenly dove in between them—but Decio's strong hand grabbed her at lightning speed and thrust her out of the way as the beasts attacked.

Out of nowhere, Kane heaved onto the field and erupted into his most fiendish form. He roared at Elena, "Run!" His voice was like thunder; his eyes surged from red to burning white as he flew. Elena jumped back. Her eyes were wide, her body in shock as she saw her father's transformation. She fell backward onto the ground. Kane looked over his shoulder and shouted at her, "Now!"

She fumbled to her feet and sped off to the castle.

Kane was by far the largest of the agramon, yet the other two had not immediately seen him arrive. Decio fought valiantly; his strength was more than the beasts had expected. Decio lunged head first into one of the beasts, sending it flying and striking the wind from it, then forced his fist into the belly of the beast, shattering whatever was beyond the surface. The monster groaned in pain and then, with one fell swoop, knocked Decio across the field.

When the two agramon looked up they were surprised to look directly into the eyes of Kane, the most dominant force of all the agramon, long thought lost or dead. Many other agramon did exist, but their blood was different, degraded; they were a subspecies, and none could measure up to the formidable force that was the fearsome dark prince—Kane.

He now stood towering and fuming. His white eyes burned right through to the hearts of the beasts, striking them with fear they had never known. The air was silent but for the snapping of

Kane's knuckles as he tightened his fists. Black
smoke flowed from his nostrils; his blood could
be seen flowing up the veins of his arms. Kane's
mind sparked with flashes of all the years gone by
that he'd suppressed this rage—years that he'd
been away from his family—resentment for this
furious anger—flashes of his sister lying there
dying because of them. He could take no more.
He opened his mouth and let out a hellacious roar
to the sky, his throat filled with the flames of Hell.
His rage would now be unleashed.

Kane rushed toward the other two agramon
and with both arms across their necks, knocked
them crashing to the ground. The earth vigorously
rumbled. He then snatched one of the agramon
with a fierce grip and tore its neck out with one
enormous crunch of his teeth. The other monster
lunged at Kane but was knocked twenty feet into
a cedar tree—and with such force it crushed the
trunk, knocking it over. As the beast got up, Kane
threw the corpse of the other agramon like a small
animal, knocking its partner to the ground once
more.

Kane stretched his arms out to the wind and
roared again. The living agramon flung the lifeless

body off of him, and watched as Kane ran for him. Just before Kane could reach him, he leapt out of the way toward Decio and sunk his teeth into the young vampire, tearing at his upper arm. Decio, now on the ground kicked the beast's stomach with incredible force, knocking the monster to the ground at the feet of Kane. Kane stomped into the chest of the agramon, crushing its bones. The sinister beast looked up into the eyes of its executioner and growled once more. Kane picked it up by the throat and separated its head from its shoulders.

Kane felt satiated, renewed. He looked over at Decio and observed his wounds. The two men stared hard into each other's eyes. Decio would be changing soon. Kane knew he should finish him off now, before it was too late. He walked closer to Decio and leaned over. He gripped the front of his shirt with his fist and began to slowly pull him upward. Decio did not struggle.

Suddenly, M'Shara appeared on her horse. "Kane, wait!" she yelled. She then jumped off of the horse and rushed to the two men. She saw that Decio had been attacked, something she'd hoped would never happen. But a thought suddenly occurred to her. "How long since he's been attacked?" she asked.

"A few minutes," Decio breathed.

M'Shara was perplexed. "And you haven't changed yet?" The effects were usually immediate. Maybe he wouldn't change at all.

Kane dropped him to the ground and turned to M'Shara. Even now, she looked at him with pure love in her eyes—even in this state, she loved him still. He couldn't believe it. His eyes began to cool and his body to calm down.

M'Shara placed her hand on his massive chest. She felt his breathing become peaceful because of her touch. He never wanted her to see him this way, yet wanted badly to hold her. But he held back, not wanting to hurt her. M'Shara moved in and softly kissed his chest, telling him that her love for him was so deep that nothing could keep her from him—and that she cherished him in any form, in any way that she could have him. She looked up into his eyes and whispered, "You are beautiful." Kane was overcome with amazement—even disbelief.

Decio watched all of this unfold. He could see the incredible bond that they shared. "I love her that way," he informed them.

The two parents quickly looked down to Decio. They knew he spoke of their daughter, and knew that if he loved her that much, they could not keep them apart. Somehow, they would have to help him survive.

CHAPTER EIGHTEEN

Standing over Decio, Kane was calm but did not completely return to his tranquil state. He was guarded because of Decio's imminent transformation. He kept a close eye on the young vampire.

M'Shara took Kane's powerful hand into hers. "My love, I've come with news. I know how to help Domnina. But we must hurry back to her. There is something you must do." M'Shara spoke in a reserved tone, but Kane noted the urgency it contained.

"Then let us go now!" he charged.

"But—what about the boy? Shall we send him to my cottage?" she asked.

Kane looked at Decio as he lay holding his bleeding arm. "No. We will take him to the dungeon. There, he will be... *secure.*"

Decio looked up into Kane's fearsome eyes. "You think I will hurt her," he stated plainly.

Kane huffed. "You won't be hurting anyone while you're locked in the depths of the citadel."

Decio stood wearily and Kane turned his body to meet him. "I would never the one I love," Decio coarsely insisted.

Kane remembered telling himself those same words long ago, but he'd grown to know better. "Your naivety could be dangerous."

Decio was furious. He boldly stepped head to chest with Kane. He spoke with utter defiance. "I will not be going to any dungeon tonight!"

Kane stood firm, but lowered his head to Decio until he was nose to nose. He enlightened Decio with a low growl. "Run... and I will enjoy hunting you."

M'Shara quickly intervened. She wedged herself between the two men until she was facing Decio. "Son, listen to me. You do not understand your condition. Please—if you truly love her, you will come with us."

Several moments of silence consumed the air. Decio finally turned to make way to the castle and Kane followed. M'Shara resisted the urge to make any comment at all to Kane. She simply bit her lip and climbed onto her horse.

At the castle, Domnina began to stir. She tossed her head from side to side and finally fluttered her eyes open. She saw black at first; she was cold but lay against something very warm. Her eyes slowly surveyed the black fabric in front of her then saw his chest. It was her LaVius. He was holding her in his arms as he sat on the edge of their bed. His magnificent hair was tied back, but was claret as it glistened in the fire's light. He lowered his face and pressed his cheek to hers as he held her tightly. His skin was warm and soothing as she faded away once more. He held her still, and felt her slip back into unconsciousness. Her heartbeat slowed to a gentle mutter. His dark heart was pained and tortured.

M'Shara and Kane took a willing Decio to the dungeon in the deepest, centermost part of the castle. He would be treated well, and the comforts of a usual chamber were ordered for his benefit, but he would not be able to escape. And he didn't want to. He didn't want to risk his reason for living, the woman with whom he wanted to spend eternity.

M'Shara and Kane made way to Domnina's bedside, where she would explain how he could help his sister. Upon entering the chamber, their eyes fell upon a tormented LaVius as he now sat in an armchair staring blankly into the fire.

"LaVius," M'Shara said quickly. "I know how to save her."

LaVius's eyes turned sharply to M'Shara. When he saw the sincerity in her eyes, he stood. "How?" he pleaded.

She turned to Kane who was equally in anguish. He grabbed her by the arms. "Tell us."

"It is risky..." M'Shara left his grasp and clasped her hands together as she walked toward her friend who lay dying. As she stared at Domnina's face she finished. "Kane... you must bite her."

The two men hollered violently in opposition.

"What do you mean bite her?" LaVius

blasted.

"M'Shara!" Kane yelled. "Do you know what I am? An agramon did this to her! She would surely die!"

Suddenly, LaVius threw himself between M'Shara and Domnina and pushed her backward into Kane. "Stay away from her!" he yelled.

Kane rushed to LaVius and the two thrust themselves eye to eye. "Don't ever touch M'Shara like that again," Kane snarled.

LaVius's eyes darkened with anger. "If either of you touches Domnina, I will do infinitely more than that," he warned.

The two men's chests heaved; their tempers began to shift into higher gear. M'Shara rolled her eyes and straightened her now disheveled cloak. She then shouted at them. "Stop this! We haven't much time! The two of you must listen to me!"

The men's eyes remained fixed on each other.

M'Shara continued. "Kane, you and Domnina share the same blood, but until now, the fierce agramon traits have only been active in you."

"Until now?" asked Kane, turning to face her.

"Yes," said M'Shara. "Your venom could enhance the strength of her inner agramon."

"This is madness, woman!" said LaVius. "You would have him turn her, which alone could kill her?"

"I do not believe she would turn," said M'Shara. "I believe the bite would simply make her stronger—more like Kane—enough to shake the toxic venom of that other beast and allow her to heal as she normally would. Believe me, LaVius—if there was any other way—"

Kane turned away. His eyes swayed back and forth. He couldn't believe what he was hearing. He could never attack Domnina. The risk was too great.

M'Shara swallowed hard. She knew this was not what anyone wanted, but it was the only way. "Kane, when you do it, your rage must be at its peak so that the venom will be its most potent."

Kane knew this could kill her. When his rage is at its worst, he can scarcely stop himself from killing. This was too dangerous. "No! I will not do it!" he roared.

LaVius came to the realization that there was no other choice. As much as he knew the risks, he also knew that the empress would surely die anyway. "Kane," LaVius began with gritted teeth, his heart in agony. "You must—or else we will lose her."

Uttering those words pierced straight through the heart of LaVius. Agreeing to this meant he might lose her now—in a matter of minutes— rather than a matter of hours or days.

This situation indeed sparked Kane's rage: his sister dying, his having to attack her. His anguish fueled his anger and his eyes turned red. Tears streamed down his face as he began to transform. His muscles tightened. His back flexed. His blood began to boil. His eyes became white.

M'Shara backed away from both men. Furious red flames could be seen in the eyes of LaVius. He couldn't watch this. He turned toward the great wooden door and with a colossal measure of strength knocked it down. And as Kane lunged at Domnina, LaVius stepped out into the corridor and roared so forcefully that it shook the boundaries of the castle and beyond.

CHAPTER NINETEEN

The deed was done. Kane had barely mustered the strength to avoid killing his sister. His teeth dripping with blood, he dropped to the floor and moaned horrifically, pounding his fist on the floor. M'Shara started toward him to console him, but he suddenly bustled outdoors. He jumped over the ledge to the balcony below and then again to the ground. He ran into the forest until his condition passed.

LaVius slowly crept back into the room. He was hesitant to look at the carnage Kane might have caused, but what he saw astonished him.

M'Shara approached the foot of the bed staring at Domnina; she was equally shocked. Domnina laid there among the white sheets, her long dark locks strewn about; her arm bloody and torn. Her dark eyes open wide and shifted between her husband and M'Shara. Her color had returned. She looked more alive than ever. She stared at them with her customary sinful gaze, but wondered why they gaped at her blankly. She raised a brow. "Do I look so dreadful?"

Abruptly they rushed to her sides. M'Shara grabbed one hand, LaVius the other. M'Shara wanted to let them be alone, but first a tear slid down her cheek. She smiled at the empress. "You're alive," she whispered. "You're alive."

Domnina didn't quite understand all of this. She had no recollection of events since riding Oblivion alongside M'Shara. She looked to LaVius for answers as M'Shara slipped away.

LaVius's eyes moved rapidly back and forth between both of Domnina's. He cupped her face with his hands. "Meus decorus diligo... my beautiful love, you have come back to me. If you'd have gone, I would have followed," he lamented, his voice languid, tender.

She closed her eyes gently and inhaled his intoxicating essence. She now understood what had happened. She'd been near death. She opened her eyes once more and stared deeply into his. "I will never leave you, my love. You are the aura of my being."

LaVius then kissed his wife, and all was right in his world.

As M'Shara took a stroll through the moonlit courtyard, she noticed her daughter nearby. "Elena," she greeted from the darkness.

Elena's eyes rose to meet her mother's. "Mother, where have you been? I've been searching for you! Father and Decio... have they returned?" she asked. "When I left them there were two agramon..."

M'Shara interrupted her. "*Were* two agramon. They are no more. And the others are gone as well."

Elena's face was washed with relief. "I'm so glad for this news."

M'Shara drew closer to Elena and bade her sit down. She placed a hand on her daughter's shoulder. "There is more. It is Decio. He has been bitten."

Elena stood quickly. "Where is he?" she cried.

"Here," M'Shara answered.

"Thank goodness. I must go to him."

"Elena," she breathed. "He is in the dungeon."

Elena's eyes grew dark. "What do you mean? Why would he be in that desolate place?" Her voice was controlled; her breath quickened.

"He is a vampire, Elena. A vampire bitten by an agramon is the most—"

"Has he changed yet?" Elena yelled. "If he had, you would have told me!"

"No... he has not."

"Then he won't! He must not have been affected! I'm going to him right now!"

M'Shara stood and tried to stop her daughter. "Wait!"

It was too late. Elena had shot off in a flash.

Just as M'Shara started after her, Kane appeared from the shadows. "M'Shara..." he hesitated. "How is she?"

M'Shara turned to him as he approached and knew immediately that he spoke of Domnina. "Oh, Kane, it is incredible news! She is—"

M'Shara paused abruptly as her eyes glimpsed movement at the top of the balcony. She smiled as she saw her friend, and turned to Kane. "Well, look for yourself." M'Shara gestured up to the terrace above.

Kane looked up and saw his sister. She stood at the stone railing next to LaVius. She wore fresh linen and was smiling brilliantly. He guffawed joyously to the sky and fell to his knees, content at last.

The four had begun to feel a sizable measure of peace, but the merriment was quickly interrupted as one of the gatekeepers came running out to the courtyard. He yelled up to LaVius and over to Kane. "Come quick! The girl is trying to break the monster free!"

Chapter Twenty

Kane and M'Shara ran hurriedly through the castle and down to the dungeon. The empress slid into a pair of suede slippers and began to follow her husband. He would take a secret corridor that would lead them there expeditiously. He turned to her with a stern gaze in an attempt to make her stay, but she gave him a disparaging look that changed his mind. There was no time to argue, so down they went.

On their way to the dungeon, the lord and empress were prepared for the worst. The gatekeeper had referred to Decio as "the monster". They knew he must have transformed. Once they arrived, LaVius secretly had a clear view into the hall of cells. It was a circular vestibule, and the shadows of flaming torches flickered on the great stone walls. The area was suspiciously quiet. He slid his hand through a crevice in the darkness and lifted a lever which opened the hidden outlet.

LaVius entered the room first to identify whether there was any threat of danger. Domnina slipped out of the corridor and began to examine the room herself. LaVius looked over his shoulder and saw her standing with her back to him. Alarmed, he turned her around to face him. "What do you think you are doing?" he asked.

"Helping you. Now let go of me," she demanded.

"Woman," he snarled. "You're barely healed. I won't have you taking such risks. Get back in the corridor."

Domnina didn't take very well to being commanded. "I will not!" she whispered forcefully. "Now unhand me and let's get back to business!"

LaVius simply reopened the door and began

to assist Domnina back through it.

"LaVius, let me go!" she huffed.

LaVius's eyes transformed into dark, blood-red pools. He slipped a dagger from his boot. Domnina was at a loss. LaVius instantly raised his hand and thrust it past his wife and into something. She ducked to the ground and turned around quickly to see him fighting an enormous, ghastly, beast. Its skin was that of slate; its eyes were blood-shot. The monster had two large fangs pointing downward, and bottom teeth that curved outward and up from its jaw.

Domnina began to feel strange. Something deep within her was beginning to emerge. She felt supremely coherent; her thoughts were crisp and clear; she could see, and feel, and hear better than ever in her life. And she could hear the pounding... the thumping of the beast's heart. She crawled across the sandy stone floor and backed up against a wall.

Suddenly, from nowhere, Decio and Elena appeared. Elena ran to Domnina, and Decio went to help LaVius. With great speed, he tore around the beast like a tornadic wind and sliced it with his teeth and claws. The animal screeched horrifically and fell to the ground.

LaVius finished it off with a thrust of his blade to the heart, and turned to Decio. He looked at him with gratitude and surprise. "Well," he began, slightly winded, "I'm glad to see you for two reasons. You were a great bit of help... and that brute wasn't you."

When Kane and M'Shara arrived, they immediately saw Decio, still in his own form—and not locked up. But they also saw Elena with Domnina who was on the ground. Domnina quickly got her bearings and stood with Elena's help. She dusted the sand and dirt from her gown before LaVius could take notice, and straightened her back as to appear normal. Kane raised his head in doubt, and kept his eyes fixed on her. He knew what was going on, but Domnina evaded his stare.

LaVius took a walk over to Elena, and Kane joined him. They noticed a dead gatekeeper lying on the ground, and the one that had come to warn them stood nearby. M'Shara kept watch on Decio and he made no moves. Elena raised her eyes to the ominous, frightening men that towered above her: her uncle, the lord of darkness, and her father, the sovereign of all agramon. She thought she should say something, but somehow words escaped her. Instead, she bit her lip.

"Why!" Kane blasted.

"How!" LaVius boomed.

"Well..." Elena honestly strained to think of the right answers.

The two men groaned; their brows turned in furiously. Abruptly, the surviving gatekeeper, known as Viscerious, approached them. "She opened two cells," he informed. "The first one was the wrong one."

LaVius and Kane shifted their eyes to the larger-than-life man in black. "And how did she do that?" LaVius asked abrasively.

"She used the key," the man answered.

LaVius's eyes burned into the man. "How did she get the key?"

LaVius, Kane, Domnina, M'Shara, and Decio all looked at Viscerious with question and awaited his response. The gigantic man looked at the floor shamefully, and barely breathed his answer. "She overpowered me."

Domnina and M'Shara smirked proudly, the

men's mouths dropped with utter shock. LaVius's eyes never left Viscerious's as he walked past him. "Get rid of the bodies. I'll deal with you later."

He'd said the last words ferociously, and Viscerious's blood went cold.

Kane then looked at Decio. "Well, it's back to the cell with you."

"No!" Elena yelled. She ran to Decio's side and they held each other.

Decio just stared deep into the eyes of Kane. "I haven't changed," he declared. "Look at me! It would have happened already."

"Yes, look at him!" Elena pleaded. "If he were going to change, he would have already, especially while fighting that beast over there that now lies dead."

Kane was not wholly convinced. He was feeling very protective of his daughter and of M'Shara, yet knew that during a fight, the beast in him would surely have made itself known.

M'Shara came over to him and turned his face to hers. "Kane, look into my eyes. I think they're right."

"But you know of the prophecy," he warned her. "There would have to be a reason for him to—" he paused hard and shot a look at his sister before finishing "—be destroyed."

"Yes, but it may have been averted," M'Shara explained.

Kane looked at LaVius to glean his feelings about all of this. LaVius looked at the ground harshly and went upstairs, leaving Kane to decide.

"Then he will stay free," Kane concluded. "Serenity help me if I'm wrong."

CHAPTER TWENTY-ONE

As the next two days passed, Elena and Decio spent most every moment together. All the while, Kane watched intensely. He followed Decio as he hunted; he watched from the veranda as the couple walked and talked. He scarcely let Decio out of his sight. His condition was too uncertain. Kane watched Decio's gestures, movements; he watched his eyes for any sign of change, but there was none. At M'Shara's urging, he tried to consider that Decio simply would not change. He wished that would be true.

The day came of the full moon, and Elena

and Decio approached the colossal doors of LaVius's sanctum. Two guards of enormous size and obvious strength sat outside the door. "Hello, gentleman," said Decio.

"Sir", one of the men answered as both guards stood up and into position.

"Might we have a word with his imperial highness?" asked Decio.

The broader man smirked. "He is not seeing anyone at this time."

"But I'm sure that if you tell him—"

"I'm sorry, sir, but I assure you it is impossible at this time," the man interrupted.

The taller of the guards growled lowly as a warning and Elena stepped in. "What are your names?" she demanded.

"Draeg," the tall one asserted.

"Draeg?" she snapped.

"Yes."

"And *your* name?" she asked the other large man.

"Kab... Kabold," he unintentionally stuttered.

"Well, Draeg and Kabold, do you value your lives?"

The two guards were frozen solid, but their

eyes turned to meet each other's. They didn't know what to think.

"I think it best if you answer me," Elena insisted. She then subtly flashed them a sideways grin, showing her sharp-looking teeth.

"Yes–yes milady," they answered.

She grinned slyly. "Then you'd better let us in to see my uncle or you'll be sorry."

"Um... uncle?" Draeg fumbled.

Elena just stared at them with wide eyes and pursed lips, as if to say, *yes, you imbeciles.*

Draeg turned to Kabold and whispered, "He said to keep *everyone* away."

Elena grew impatient. "I'm waiting!"

The two men turned further away and toward the double oak doors with their whispers.

"But you heard her. She said he was her uncle. Do you think that makes a difference?" Kabold wondered aloud.

Draeg inhaled deeply. "I don't know about this. I think it best if we stick precisely to his instructions," he concluded. "Otherwise, he'll have our heads—or worse."

Elena had enough of waiting. "So, are you letting us in or what?"

"No," the two men said in unison, and then swallowed hard just in case they were making a grave mistake.

The doors began to open slowly, and Lord LaVius himself stood behind the two men with a stern look. They stood firm and didn't turn around to see it. "It is very wise of you to follow my orders," spoke LaVius in a low tone.

Draeg and Kabold let a silent sigh of relief until LaVius continued, "But a mistake to interrupt me with your murmuring."

The two men turned to him, their backs stiff, their spears tall, and apologized. LaVius sighed with frustration, and then his eyes fell upon the young couple. "What is it you two require of me?" he asked.

"Please, my lord. If we may—speak to you privately?" Decio cordially requested.

"Very well," LaVius obliged. "Come in and sit."

They followed his instruction and entered the massive room. The two guards closed the doors and sighed so deeply with reprieve that LaVius heard them and rolled his eyes.

The room was tall, wide, and circular. Part of

the wall was stone, carved to look like the bark and limbs of an enormous tree, and held books, papers, and scrolls of many sizes. Everything was perfectly organized; not a thing looked out of place. Murals were painted on the remaining wall around the fireplace and on the ceiling. The images were of magical creatures of all types, and a mist that surrounded them like shadows; at the top the colors were warm, at the bottom they were bluish-green and cool. LaVius sat behind a very large desk that looked as if it were carved from one solid trunk of a tree. It was oblong, and there were three legs on each side that looked like those of a wild animal. "What is it you want?" LaVius asked.

Decio gripped Elena's hand and smiled. "We wish to be married tonight," he answered.

LaVius was not surprised, but even he had dreaded this moment. He knew Kane was against this even now, and had no desire to go against his wishes. "And why do you come to me with this?" he grumbled.

Elena jumped to her feet and rushed to his desk. "Because you can marry us," she blurted, and stared at him with pleading eyes.

"I see you've taken leave of your senses," said LaVius. "I will not go against your father's wishes."

"But you must! We are in love!"

"I mustn't do anything," he informed her.

"Even if the empress asks you too?" Elena asked sweetly.

"Domnina would do no such thing."

"Even for true love?" the empress asked as she entered with M'Shara—to LaVius's great surprise.

LaVius inhaled sharply. "What is the meaning of this, woman?" he questioned. "You do not seriously expect me go along with this. I will not be moved."

The empress closed the doors behind them. She was dressed in a flowing white evening gown; her dark hair was up and rippling tresses hung down and framed her face. She was the picture of her glowing, healthy self. M'Shara wore deep plum velvet that flowed like silk. Her hair was sculpted into a beautiful bouquet of curls, with just the slightest hint of auburn to warm them. Both women were a vision. LaVius knew they were dressed for an occasion and groaned knowingly. His chest grew tight, his jaw clenched. He stood dauntingly, his fists ground into the desk.

The two women went over to him and each placed a hand on his shoulder gently. He ignored their pleading eyes. He stared forward and grumbled, "Your womanly wiles are of no consequence." He then turned his eyes shiftily to his wife. "I said, I will not be moved," he reminded her.

She smirked. "Oh, LaVius! See reason!"

"When have I heard *that* before?" he jested.

M'Shara laughed to herself.

Suddenly, the doors blasted open. It was Kane. "What is going on in here?" he demanded.

In the doorway, all one could see of the guards was the bottoms of their feet as they laid on the ground unconscious.

LaVius closed his eyes tight. "I need better help," he said.

CHAPTER TWENTY-TWO

Kane stood in the doorway fuming. His jaw was tight; his chest heaved visibly beneath the red tunic that was untied to his waist. He wore black pants and tall boots and stood there looming, angrily.

M'Shara wanted to go to Kane with this first. However, she knew she and Domnina would have to get LaVius on board to help put Kane's mind at ease about the situation. Neither idea was going according to plan.

LaVius simply scoffed at the women as he sat. He then turned his eyes to his wife's brother.

"Kane, I assure you, I had no part in this." He leaned forward onto his desk. "They tried," he informed him while looking at the other four who stood in the room. "But it was a fruitless effort."

Domnina's eyes glowered at him as he sat back comfortably in his chair and folded his hands. He just smirked.

She then turned to her brother. "Kane, all we want is for you to accept this."

His eyes widened with genuine surprise. "Accept this? Accept this!" he roared. He looked as if he would implode.

M'Shara hurried over to him. "Kane, please..." she begged, and tried to hold his arms as they were flailing around. "Kane, look at me."

He did look at her. He stared directly into her eyes and through to her soul. "You went behind my back." His tone was solid, forceful, and deep.

"Kane, it wasn't that way, I swear to you. I only wanted to see if LaVius would—"

"No!" Kane blasted. "I won't hear any more of this." He went over to Decio and grabbed him by the throat. He wanted to make him change. He was going to force the beast to emerge. The women screamed.

"No, Kane, no! Stop this! Please!" M'Shara pleaded.

Elena tried to break her father's grip to no avail. "Father, no!"

In defense, Decio blasted his strong hands into Kane's chest forcing him many feet back. The vampire's eyes began to redden. Elena jumped between the men, but Decio shoved her out of the way.

Kane's lips curved into a satisfied grin as he stared the younger man down. "Yes," he drawled. "Let it come. Release the beast. I know it's in there." His eyes too became red and Domnina and M'Shara knew this was about to take a terrible turn.

Domnina slinked over to her brother and whispered, "Kane."

LaVius went over to the doors that led to the sunlit grounds. He pressed them open and moved to the side. Kane then punched the vampire with such force that thrust him outside. Elena ran after them. The fight had begun.

Domnina and M'Shara stared at LaVius crossly, then went out the door. All they could do was watch the carnage unfold. They too knew this was the only way.

They watched as Decio put up a valiant fight. His strength was immense, his speed unparalleled. Kane beat him, and flung him, and choked the young immortal. Decio stood his own, and fought with terrific force, but no beast would emerge from him. Kane was relentless; he would not give up until Decio's inner agramon was revealed. The clashes from the fight frightened the wildlife from the trees, and rumbled the earth for nearly a league.

Finally, Kane stood still and wiped the blood from his lip. He breathed huskily. Decio's shirt had been torn from him. While his pale skin was vivid in the sun, his muscles contracted, and his jaw clenched, but both men sensed the fight was over.

Kane walked right up to Decio and firmly gripped his shoulder. "Then you shall marry my daughter. But I'll be watching you." His eyes flickered white then back to their normal shade. It would serve as a reminder to Decio of the beast within his bride's father; a reminder that he didn't need, for he'd seen Kane tear apart two other agramon.

M'Shara and Elena ran and threw their arms around Kane. Domnina sighed with relief that this was over and latched on to her husband's arm. He raised a brow and looked down at her. "I suppose there will be a wedding after all," he remarked wryly.

"I suppose there will," she smiled. "And tonight's the night."

Chapter Twenty-Three

The grandest room in the citadel was Brimstone Hall. It was incredibly vast. Enormous stone columns curved up high, and the ceiling was open to the elements of the night sky. As night began to fall, many folks gathered there. Word had been given that the emperor required their presence, and all who were invited attended without question of the late notice.

The imperial lord waited at the end of the long hall. He sat upon a large throne atop eleven marble stairs that curved outward facing the assembly. He wore a leather frock coat, the color of night. His luxurious hair was pulled backward on the top and sides and was secured neatly at the back of his head; the length of his hair remained long and draped over his broad shoulders. His demeanor was serious; his lips were still. Kane stood beside him, tall and dark. His garb was entirely black; his shirt was tucked; his jacket was long and velvet. Both men were fiercely handsome, and together were an incomparably ominous presence.

Decio entered and was regally dressed. He knelt on one leg on the stair before LaVius and bowed. Before rising, however, he raised his eyes to Kane searching for any sign of approval. Both men spoke only with their gaze. Kane was ever cautious of the young vampire.

The empress appeared next to LaVius, signifying the bride was ready to begin. She kept her place at his side, and signaled with a nod for the bard to begin their gentle melody. M'Shara appeared with Elena on her arm. LaVius raised his hands slowly telling the guests to rise.

When Decio saw Elena, she took his breath away. Kane took note of this. He then turned his eyes to his daughter and was equally taken aback.

She was clad in sapphire silk from her neck to her feet, and encircling her waist a magnificent girdle of gold and mother of pearl, a wedding gift from the empress herself. Kane was overcome with emotion. His beautiful child; he'd watched her blossom over the years into a determined, vibrant, and beautiful lady—just like her mother.

As the harpists played, the bride and her mother drew near. Kane gazed at the two women and slowed his breath in attempt to conceal his feelings. He'd only felt such emotion two other times in his existence; the first was when M'Shara reentered his life, the second was the first time his daughter, now grown, had smiled when she looked into his eyes. M'Shara knew the truth of his feelings when she saw his endearing gaze, and she smiled.

Decio took Elena's hands and exhaled. His heart was filled with love and longing for her, and her alone. They had longed for this moment. They had conquered countless tribulations to reach this point. Elena stared lovingly into his eyes and breathed his essence into her own. The smiles on their lips were those of genuine love and devotion. Kane saw this and realized he had made the right decision—the only decision. He would never again stand in their way. M'Shara went to Kane's side at the top of the short staircase, and LaVius walked down and began the ceremony.

Lord LaVius wished the couple prosperity and for their love to endure. He spoke many words in an ancient tongue that seemed to seal the vows. Closing, LaVius officially pronounced their union and Decio dipped his bride gently in his arms as they kissed.

Suddenly, it began to snow. Soft downy flakes of the purest white fluttered onto the joyous scene and whitened the entire hall. The crowd cheered and every soul was filled with merriment.

M'Shara smiled brightly and began to descend the snowy stairs past LaVius and toward the young couple. She thought that Kane had followed. But suddenly LaVius stopped her with his words. "We are not finished yet, M'Shara."

M'Shara paused and turned to look at him. She searched his eyes for reason. Elena and Decio smiled and backed away slowly and knowingly. M'Shara didn't understand. Then Kane descended the staircase. His dark attire and alluring frame were brilliant against the backdrop of the fallen snow.

He extended his hand to M'Shara. She placed her hand in his and he pulled her close to him. "M'Shara, you are my life. You are the sun that warms my skin, the light that guides my path. You are everything to me, and I should have done this a long time ago." He kissed her lips softly. "Will you be my wife?"

M'Shara felt weak. She was overwhelmed. She hadn't expected this and wanted nothing more than to be his wife. "Forever," she said with a warm smile. He breathed a noticeable sigh of relief. She reached for his face and pulled him to her lips in a fervent kiss.

"Eh-hem… shall we begin?" asked LaVius.

They simply continued to kiss.

CHAPTER TWENTY-FOUR

Kane and M'Shara were married as the full moon rose high above the snowy realm. The feelings they had always shared were rich with intensity; they'd always felt bound to each other in every way. In their hearts they were already married, but this night, they felt replete with passionate oneness, they felt whole, complete.

The lord and empress stood on the balcony that overlooked the guests in the hall. They knew there was one special guest that had attended but had remained out of sight. They felt him there.

One was always aware of his presence. He wished to speak with Domnina in a private chamber and she knew this.

Suddenly, she felt it was time. LaVius knew it as well. He turned to her before she walked away and pulled her close. He spoke softly as he brushed his fingers against her neck. "If you need me…" he began.

Domnina invited his mouth to hers. She eagerly tasted his lips. "I always need you, my lord," she said truthfully. "But, don't worry about me. I can handle him well enough."

LaVius grinned. "It is him I worry about."

She smiled and took leave.

As Domnina entered the underground corridor she saw the doorway of the room she approached. Underneath, it was glowing with the reds and yellows of the roaring fireplace. It lighted the hallway and she noticed someone else approaching from the opposite direction. They met outside the room. "You felt him too, brother?"

"Yes. I felt him beckoning us both."

"Shall we?" she huffed as they entered the room.

There he sat in LaVius's large chair watching the fire intently. When the two entered, he turned quickly and gave them a genuine, yet sinister smile. "My, my. I haven't seen you two together in a very long time. It truly warms my heart."

Kane groaned. "Where is this heart you speak of, Lucifer?"

The man shifted in his seat and his eyes grew dark. "We're using formal names now, are we?"

"What is it you want, father?" Domnina demanded.

"Oh, dear. I must have really upset the both of you. First, I wasn't invited to the gala tonight, and now this insolence. What is it I have done?" he asked, feigning innocence.

Kane inhaled deeply and turned to the fireplace. He leaned one arm on the heavy mantle. Domnina poured them each a drink and gave their father his while raising a suspicious brow. "We know that you want something," she informed him.

"So suspicious," he retorted. "Fine. If you must know, I simply came to give my regards… and to give you some news."

"We're listening," Kane grumbled.

"The prophecy has been altered. It seems circumstances have... well, *changed*." He took a good long drink of the fiery liquid Domnina had poured and watched as Kane and Domnina looked at each other in disbelief. They then turned to him cautiously.

Kane was especially vigilant. "How do you mean?"

"Something you've done has changed things. The boy won't kill anyone tonight, and thus M'Shara won't destroy him. So, you have nothing to worry about."

While Lucifer was talking, Elena had entered the room. She'd been searching for her father to tell him goodbye and heard what Lucifer had just said. She stood bewildered. "'M'Shara'?" she mouthed barely above a whisper. "You told me it was you, Domnina. You would be the one..." She could hardly stand.

Kane and Domnina went to her side and braced her. As her father held her up, she regained her strength and turned to Domnina. "You were protecting her," she realized. "You lied to me... but you were protecting her."

Kane and Domnina didn't know if she was

angry or saddened. Kane turned her to face him. "Elena, it's of no consequence now. The prophecy has been altered. Don't be upset."

She surprised them both. "I am not upset." She returned her gaze to Domnina. "I'm thankful. I spent many years defiant of you, never knowing you were family, and never knowing you could care so much. I see so many things differently now." She looked at both her father and Domnina, still in wonder. "I have learned a lot since I returned, and I still have a lot to learn. Thank you both for everything you've done."

Elena suddenly embraced Domnina for the first time. When she looked up, Lucifer opened his arms and said with pride, "And I am your grandfather."

Elena put up a finger in pause and said, "Not quite ready for that yet."

Kane placed his hand on his sister's shoulder and they both grinned as they watched Elena leave.

Lucifer was incensed. "You enjoyed that, didn't you, Kane?"

"Immensely. Are we finished here, old man?" Kane questioned authoritatively.

Lucifer huffed and placed his drink on a table. "I suppose so, since I'm not wanted."

The siblings rolled their eyes.

"It's just as well," he went on. "I'm going on a trip. I'm going to lure some unsuspecting new recruits."

Domnina sneered at him. "You know how we feel about your 'recruiting'. There is no need for trickery. You just like to play unnecessary games."

"But it's so much fun!" He grinned slyly and rubbed his hands together.

"What will you be this time?" Kane asked smugly. "A schoolmaster?"

"No, no. How dull. This time I will be a jeweler, under the guise of Jim Stone. Get it? *Djim*-Stone? Eh, you never had a sense of humor."

Kane was not amused.

Domnina glared at their father with a sinister smile. "Play these games if you will—for now. Things will be much different when I am in command."

This enraged him and she knew it. He burst into a giant tower of roaring flames, his massive horns and piercing eyes apparent. "Don't cross me young lady!" he boomed.

Kane and Domnina simply walked out the door, unmoved by his theatrics, and closed it behind them.

He shook off his flames, changing back into his human-looking self and poured himself another drink. "Children. Absolutely no respect."

CHAPTER TWENTY-FIVE

Kane and Domnina made their way to the main foyer of the castle where Decio and Elena were about to leave. LaVius had summoned for them one of the royal carriages. It was crafted of ebony, with black curtains, and horses with jet coats pulled it behind them. It was not meant to be seen, only heard. The driver relied on his keen sense of clairvoyance to lead the way as was done with all of the dark lord's carriages that traveled by night.

Elena and M'Shara were happy to see Kane return. Kane kissed them both on the foreheads.

"How are you two?" he asked, knowing they must have discussed what Elena had overheard.

M'Shara held her daughter tighter. "We are sublime," she smiled. "What of your father? Did it go well?"

Kane groaned slightly. "As well as always," he answered. "My father is up to his evil ways again."

Elena smiled. "Uh, lord of the netherworld," she reminded him.

"I suppose you're right," he grinned. The others were humored, particularly the lord and empress.

Decio choked back his chortle then took Elena by the arm. "Your chariot awaits milady," he said softly.

Kane looked Decio over one last time. A lot had happened in recent days. First, and most importantly, his family was back together. The second probing fact was that Decio had been bitten by a pure agramon; a detail that Kane would always be mindful of. Decio's eyes slowly rose to meet Kane's. Both men knew what crisis had been averted. They knew the horrific connotations of a vampire marked with agramon blood. But remarkably, he had made it through unscathed. Kane was deep in thought.

M'Shara took careful notice of this and gently linked her husband's arm with hers. He broke his gaze and looked down at her. His heart was filled with pure love.

"Kane, everything is all right now—isn't it?" she asked.

He was in a trance for several moments as his soul drank her in. "Yes," he said. As he regained hold of his bearings, he realized she was referring to the news his father had brought about the prophecy. "I mean, yes, yes, everything is fine tonight." He then brushed his thumb against her smooth cheek.

Domnina was happy for her brother. It had been too long since she'd seen any peacefulness in him. She smiled to herself and went over to usher the newlywed vampires out the door. "We'll see you two very soon of course," she reminded the couple.

"Of course, your grace," Decio replied. Always the gentleman, he then bowed slightly and kissed her hand and then M'Shara's. "Please know that my cold heart is sincerely warmed by the generosity and confidence your family has bestowed upon me. And I am truly humbled to have Elena in my life. I swear to love her for all of my days."

Elena's mother and aunt took this in graciously, as Kane and LaVius looked at each other and spoke without words. Elena and Decio then slipped into the carriage and it rode away.

Kane turned to LaVius. "We will be leaving as well."

LaVius was somewhat surprised. "Kane, my castle is yours; there is no reason for you to go."

"Then we will go for a short while, to be together, to make up for lost time," he smiled at his lovely woman. "Then, if my wife wishes, we shall return." M'Shara grinned lovingly into Kane's inviting eyes.

To Domnina's surprise, LaVius held her a little tighter as they observed this romantic interlude. LaVius felt that Kane's love for M'Shara might even be close to what he felt for his own bride.

"Domnina," said LaVius in a low tone. "Your father said the prophecy had changed, but you never told me what it changed *to*," he remarked.

The empress squinted and thought back to

that meeting. "He didn't say."

The couple watched as Kane and his bride took leave. Such jubilance and tenderness had not ever graced the walls of the dark castle. While glad for the newlywed couples, both the lord and empress silently yearned for a speedy return to normalcy.

Deep in the dark forest, the full moon flickered between the snowy trees as the carriage rode. Decio and Elena sat in the back never minding the little bumps and wide turns, only savoring each other's loving embrace. "We are finally together," said Decio.

Elena smiled and laid her head comfortably on his chest. "Yes. And nothing shall ever come between us."

Decio held her even closer. He kissed her hair as he stared through the window. As the moments passed, he desperately tried to fight it, but something was brewing deep within him. His blood began to simmer. His eyes burned as they turned a blazing red. He knew something was terribly wrong. Elena broke from his grasp and began to heave heavily as she stared deeply into his questioning eyes. A low growl began to emerge from within her, the carriage began to tremble. And then, in an irrepressible, violently painful instant—*her eyes turned white.*

EPILOGUE

"The carriage was not just overturned," said a guard to Domnina. "It was hardly recognizable. It's been torn wholly apart. No one is there to be found, not even the driver, Carrick. Word has been sent to the girl's parents as Lord LaVius instructed."

Domnina pondered this. She dismissed the man and went deep into thought. "Decio," she said aloud. "It couldn't be. He was tested so. It isn't possible."

"No, it is not," said LaVius, upon entering the candlelit room. "We both know it is Elena." He caressed his wife's face with his hands and stared lovingly into her eyes.

"Yes," said Domnina. "She is both vampire and agramon; a dangerous combination that we'd hoped would never be a problem for the girl."

LaVius pulled Domnina close and she laid her head on his chest. "I thought she'd be protected by her mother's blood," she said, sliding her arms around him and holding him tight. "I am afraid this will not end well. Her bloodthirst and rage will be uncontrollable," she lamented. "She must be captured and—"

LaVius finished for her, "dealt with as necessary. However, disagreeable."

His wife was less firm in her conviction. With some effort she was able to reply, "Yes."

"Domnina, there is more to this than a girl stricken with a violent affliction," warned LaVius.

Domnina raised her head and looked into his eyes. "What do you mean?" she asked.

"Half a dozen agramon didn't appear out of the ethers," he said.

Domnina had been preoccupied with family matters and with healing after having been attacked. She'd never thought further about the agramon until now. "You're right LaVius. What will we do?"

"You will stay here," he said, taking her hand and leading her to the balcony. "Govern your realm as usual. Be watchful and aware."

The balcony was high in the castle; and from where they stood, they could see beyond the vast forests and to the distant sea of dark hills and mountain silhouettes. This time, when Domnina looked into her husband's eyes, she saw memories. Memories of the fields of lavender that reside among those hills and mountains; and of the valleys and meadows where they've ridden their horses together and made love under the blue skies and blazing sun. The image in his eyes then changed. She saw dark clouds and lightning, and they were together on a distant plane. It was memory of long ago. They were escorting souls to an outer world known as Darkness; a realm between the first and final dimensions; where some souls go before they begin again.

"You're going to see my father."

"Yes," said LaVius. "And also, to the Gaiamne, to discuss many things."

Domnina knew the wisdom in this. The Gaiamne dwelled in a different outer world than her father; a neutral plane. They served as council to all keepers and as guardians of knowledge and history.

LaVius and Domnina kissed. Passion and love burned inside them. Each second, their bodies filled with rapture; a constant reminder that their own souls were bound to one another for eternity. Before leaving her embrace, he whispered, "I'll return to you, my love."

"Quickly," said Domnina, letting her fingers trail down his chest.

When he turned to go, she stopped him. "What about Elena?"

"The hounds will find her," he replied.

READ NEXT

THE SHIFTY SERVANTS,
AN ADVENTURE TALE OF THE VALOR OF WOMEN

EMERALD ISLE, A PARANORMAL ROMANCE,
A DANGEROUS LEGEND MEETS ITS MATCH IN A
TALE OF UNWAVERING TRUE LOVE

For more information
about these and other titles,
visit www.MariaChristineOnline.com
and www.NocturnaPress.com